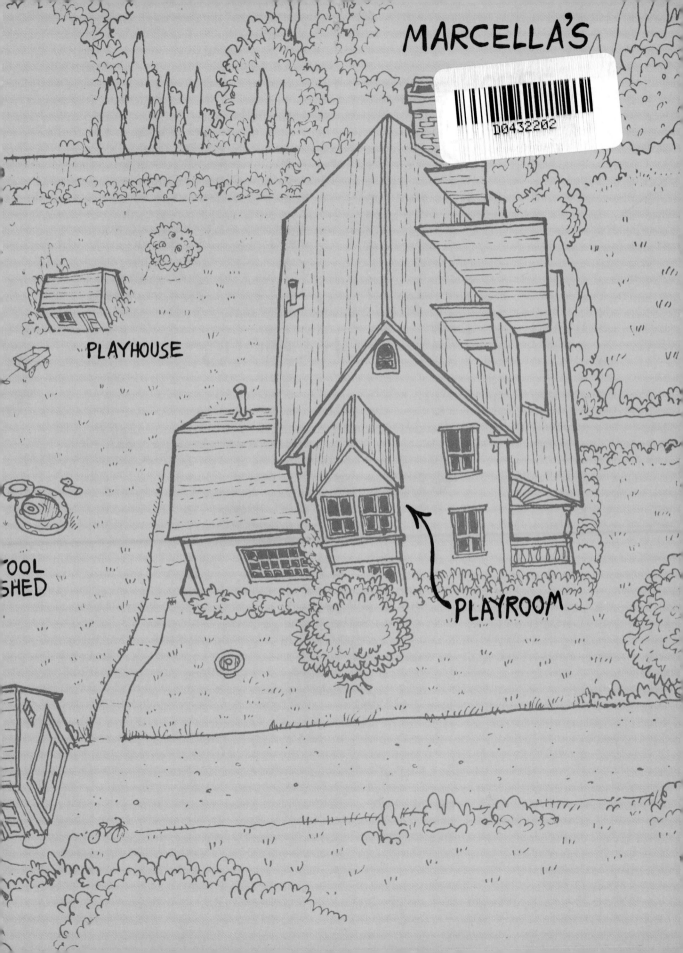

This book belongs to:

Aleksandra

Raggedy Ann & Andy's

GROW
AND
LEARN
LIBRARY

VOLUME 2

LITTLE BEAR'S PROBLEM

A LYNX BOOK

One morning, Marcella rushed into the playroom.
"Raggedy Ann! Raggedy Andy! I have some wonderful
news," Marcella told her dolls. "We're going to visit my
friend George. You'll never guess where!"

"George works with his father at the circus!" Marcella said as she hugged the Raggedys. "And he's invited us to come and visit!"

In no time at all, Marcella and the Raggedys arrived at the circus. Marcella knew exactly where to meet George and his father, the animal trainer.

The animal show was about to begin.

"Remember to feed the bear cub," George's father reminded him as he left for the show.

"Would you like to help me get the food for the bear cub?" George asked Marcella.

"I'd love to," Marcella answered happily.

"You'll have to leave your dolls here while we're gone. They'll be all right till we get back," George promised.

So Marcella gently placed Raggedy Ann and Raggedy Andy on a box. "I'll be back soon," she whispered softly. Then she and George skipped off to get food for the bear cub and to see some of the circus.

"Oh, Raggedy Andy! Isn't the circus a wonderful place?" Raggedy Ann exclaimed.

"It sure is! Just look at those juggling clowns—and those acrobats on the trapeze!" Raggedy Andy said. "Boy, I think the circus is the greatest place in the whole world."

"That's what everyone thinks," said a sad little voice from the bear cage. "Everyone except me, that is."

"Who said that?" asked Raggedy Andy.

"I did," answered a bear cub sitting in the corner of the bear cage. "I'm Little Bear."

"Do you mean that you *really* don't like the circus?"
Raggedy Andy asked Little Bear.
   "That's right," the cub replied.
   "But why not?" Raggedy Ann asked gently.

"Because my parents are always so busy working for the circus. They have to practice their silly old tricks every day. And they hardly have any time for me!" complained Little Bear.

"You mean you get to watch them do their circus tricks every day?" asked Raggedy Andy. "Gosh, you don't know how lucky you are!"

Raggedy Ann had listened carefully to the bear cub's words. "Do you mean your parents don't have time to do nice things with you, like tell you stories?" Raggedy Ann asked.

"They tell me stories at nap time and at bedtime every day," said Little Bear quickly.

"Perhaps they don't have enough time to play any games with you?" asked Raggedy Ann, trying hard to understand just what was troubling Little Bear.

"Oh, they do play games with me, in between practicing their tricks and on their days off," he admitted.

"I don't understand!" said Raggedy Andy. "Your parents tell you stories. They play games with you. And they're in the circus! What are you so unhappy about, Little Bear?"

"I just hate it when my parents leave me here to go off to do their show. Why can't they stay here with me all the time? I think this dumb old circus is more important to them than I am," Little Bear said angrily.

Now the Raggedys both understood. Little Bear wanted his parents to pay more attention to him.

"I've never seen your parents' circus act," said Raggedy Ann, trying to cheer up the bear cub. "Do you think you could show us what they do?" she asked.

And Little Bear tried, but he couldn't do many of the tricks. "The tricks take lots of practice," he explained.

"Can your parents do all those tricks without making any mistakes?" asked Raggedy Andy in a very impressed voice.

"They can do the tricks during practice without any mistakes," the bear cub answered. "But I've never seen them do their show."

"Why not?" asked Raggedy Andy.

"I'm not allowed to go out and sit with the people," Little Bear explained. "And the tent flap is always closed back here."

Raggedy Ann jumped up. "I have the perfect plan!" she cried. "Raggedy Andy and I can pull back the tent flap, and the three of us can watch your parents' show together. Hurry, Raggedy Andy, I hear the ringmaster saying that the bears are about to go on!"

From their special seats, the Raggedys and Little Bear
watched Little Bear's parents tumble and roll into the ring.

Next the two bears danced a sweet little dance.
"They do that dance with me sometimes," Little Bear whispered proudly.

Then the bears climbed on top of two big circus balls and each balanced a small ball on the tip of its nose.

"That's a really hard trick," Little Bear told Raggedy Ann and Raggedy Andy. "My parents have to practice that one every day!"

"Gee, I've never seen them ride their bicycles like that before! Aren't they great?" Little Bear asked happily.

"Oh, yes. They're wonderful!" Raggedy Ann agreed. "And they both look so proud," she added.

"Just listen to that crowd cheer!" said Raggedy Andy. "I wish I could make people cheer like that for me!"

"And they make so many people happy!" Raggedy Ann added.

"Hey, look at me," called Little Bear, scrambling up onto a ball. "I can do tricks just like my parents can!"

PLOP! Little Bear slipped right off the ball onto the ground.

"I think you need a little more practice!" laughed Raggedy Ann.

"You know something, Raggedy Ann?" Little Bear asked thoughtfully. "When I grow up, I want to work in the circus, too. So I'm going to practice real hard, just like my mom and dad."

Raggedy Ann wanted to tell the bear cub how glad she was that he understood at last about his parents and their work. But before she could say another word, Raggedy Andy called out, "Quick—Marcella is coming!"

"Oh, my! The bears are the best part of the circus," Marcella told George as they came back carrying food for the bear cub. "And this little bear certainly seems hungry!" she said as she fed him his lunch.

"He must like the way that you feed him," said George. "He hasn't been very hungry or happy for the last few days."

"Well, he seems pretty happy now!" Marcella said with a laugh. And she fed the little bear until George's father returned. Then it was time to go home.

HANDLE WITH CARE

"Thank you for inviting us," Marcella said. "You're so lucky to work at the circus—and to work with your father, too! See you next time, George," Marcella called.

As Marcella walked away, she hugged the Raggedys close to her. "You poor dears. You didn't get to see any of the show. The next time I come, I'll make sure that you do!" And at that, Raggedy Ann and Raggedy Andy just smiled.

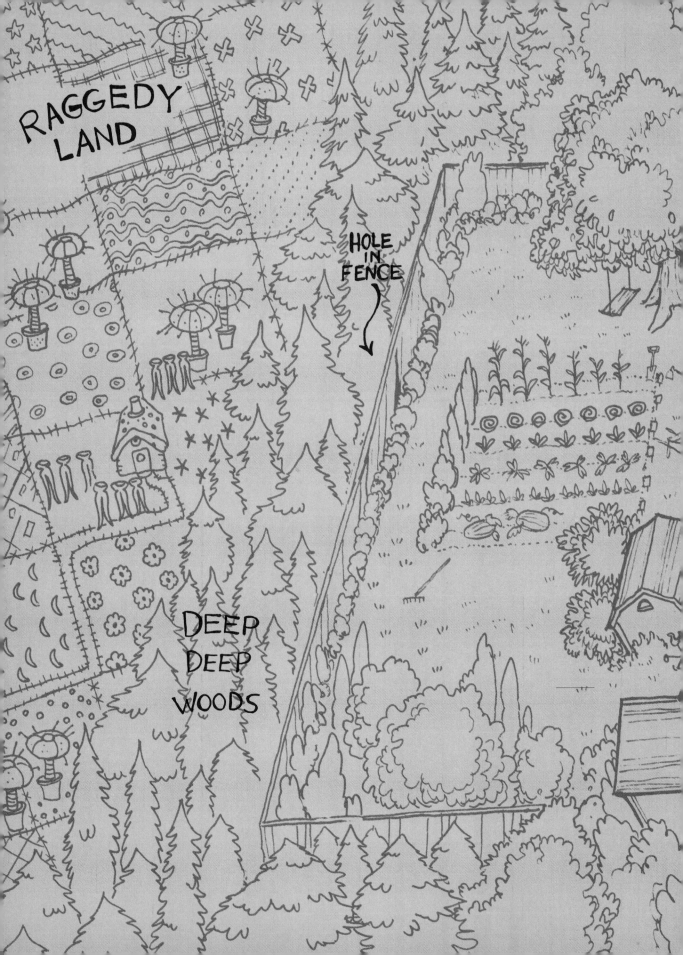